TINY TIMMY

ON HOLIDAY!

TO _____

FOLLOW YOUR DREAMS!

A Scholastic Australia Book

To Oli,

I can't wait until you're old enough to read this yourself.

Until then, I know your big brothers will help! Love always, uncle Tim.

Scholastic Australia
345 Pacific Highway Lindfield NSW 2070
An imprint of Scholastic Australia Pty Limited
PO Box 579 Gosford NSW 2250
ABN 11 000 614 577
www.scholastic.com.au

Part of the Scholastic Group
Sydney • Auckland • New York • Toronto • London • Mexico City
• New Delhi • Hong Kong • Buenos Aires • Puerto Rico

Published by Scholastic Australia in 2018.
Text copyright © Scholastic Australia, 2018.
Text by Tim Cahill and Julian Gray.
Illustrations copyright © Scholastic Australia, 2018.
Illustrations by Heath McKenzie.

A catalogue record for this
book is available from the
National Library of Australia

NATIONAL
LIBRARY
OF AUSTRALIA

Typeset in Mozzart Sketch and Bizzle Chizzle.

Printed in Australia by Griffin Press.
Scholastic Australia's policy, in association with Griffin Press, is to use
papers that are renewable and made efficiently from wood grown in
responsibly managed forests, so as to minimise its environmental footprint.

18 19 20 21 22 / 1

CHAPTER 1

There isn't much time left. I can feel the seconds ticking away. If this is going to happen, **it has to happen now**!

I looked over at Coach Roach. He nodded to me, as if to say, **'You can do it.'** I nodded back.

I took some deep breaths. **'This is what you've practised all those hours for,'** I said to myself.

Flip the pages to see me in action!

I heard someone call out, 'One minute to go!'

It was now or never! If I messed up here, there **wouldn't be another chance**.

I had to make a decision. _Fast!_

I worked out just what I wanted to do, **then I made my move**.

'The answer is definitely "B",' I said as I coloured in the circle with my pencil.

'Time's up,' said Coach Roach. 'Pencils down, everyone.'

I sat back in my chair, **totally exhausted**!

'Wow, those multiple choice tests **<u>aren't easy</u>**,' said Sienna as we walked out into the playground.

'You're not wrong about that!' said Mike.

Hacker and Studs were walking past. **'As if!'** said Studs. 'They're the **simplest exams** there are! And that one just now was the **easiest one yet**, right Hacker?'

'Yeah, actually **too easy**. I was finished with plenty of time to spare,' said Hacker.

Studs continued, 'Even if you didn't know all the answers—'

'And we **<u>definitely</u> did!**' interrupted Hacker.

'But even if you didn't,' Studs went on, 'you can still **take a guess**! What kind of test is that?!'

'**An easy one,**' said Hacker. 'And here's a tip: whenever you're not sure, **go with "C"**,' he said with a wink.

And with that, Studs and Hacker **went off to stomp the ground** in front of some pigeons so they'd get scared and fly off.

'Anyway . . .' I said, **shaking my head** at Hacker and Studs, 'I think I did pretty well in the test. And even better—**that's the last one for the term!** Only four more days until—'

'SCHOOL HOLIDAYS!' shouted everyone.

'Yeah!' I said. 'What's everybody doing?'

'I'm going with my family to **see my grandparents in China**!' said Millie.

'Wow, awesome!' said Mike. 'I'm staying home, but I'll definitely be **going to the park every day** to work on my soccer skills. Who wants to come along?'

'I'm not going away or anything,' said Ricardo, 'so **I'll be there for sure**!'

'That sounds great,' said Sienna, 'but I'm actually **going away to soccer camp**. We'll be eating, breathing and playing soccer all day for two whole weeks! I can't wait! Tim, do you know yet if you can come too?'

'No, **I keep asking every day** but Mum and Dad still haven't said if I can go or not,' I said. 'I really want to, but if I can't I'll definitely be at the park with you guys every day, Mike and Ricardo!'

'**How good will that be?!**' said Mike. 'Just like lunchtime at school, but **all day, every day**!'

We all gave each other a big high five.

'Hopefully tonight I'll find out what I'm doing,' I said. 'Either way, it's going to be the **best school holidays ever**!'

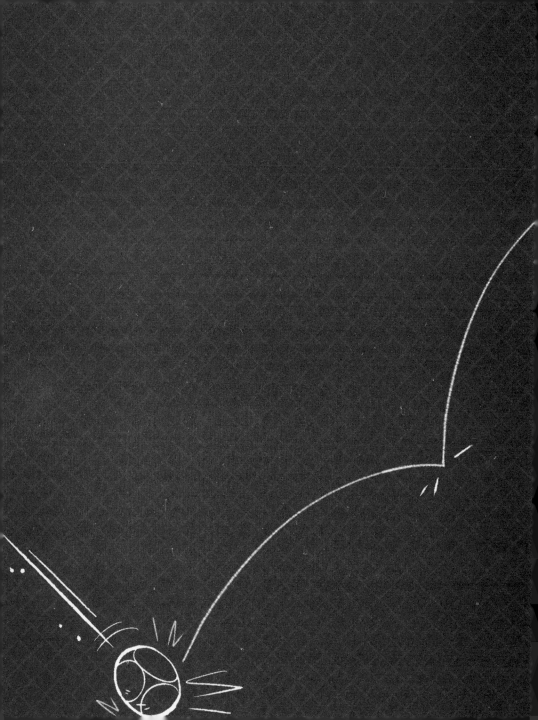

CHAPTER 2

When I got home from school, the **first thing** I did was ask Mum again if I could go to the soccer camp in the holidays.

'Hold on a minute,' Mum said. 'How was your test today at school?'

At this rate **the camp was going to be over before I knew if I was even allowed to go to it**!

'Good, I think,' I said. '**I prepared as well as I could,** so I'm happy about that. And we won't get the results back until after the holidays, so there's no point worrying about it now. **Can I go to the camp?**'

'Your dad's going to let you know about that at dinnertime,' Mum said.

Oh... **That <u>didn't</u> sound like it was going to be good news!** If I was allowed to go, Mum surely would have told me here and now!

Just then, Kyah and Shae came running into the kitchen. They hadn't had any tests at school to worry about, so they'd been looking forward to the holidays for ages. And **counting down the days**—literally!

There was a big calendar on the fridge, and Kyah walked over and put a cross through today. **'Only four days to go!'** he said, and he and Shae did **a little holiday dance**. 'Can't wait!'

'So boys, looking forward to the holidays?' asked Dad when dinner was nearly finished.

'Yeah!' we all shouted.

'Well, **I've got a surprise** for you,' Dad went on. **'Any guesses** as to what we'll be doing?'

'Am I going to the soccer camp?' I asked, excited.

'**Afraid not,**' said Dad, 'but I think you'll like what we're doing instead.'

I was disappointed, but I didn't want to show it.

'I know what we're doing,' said Shae, very sure of himself. '**We're all going to . . . the WORLD CUP!** I'm right, aren't I?!'

'The **WORLD CUP** was just on!' said Kyah. 'The next one isn't for four more years, so it definitely can't be that!'

Now it was Shae's turn to be disappointed. But not for long, because he had another guess, and he **seemed very sure** about this one, too!

'**We're going to Mars in a rocket,**' Shae said, nodding to himself. 'We'll be the first family to **play a game of soccer in space**! That's definitely what we're doing, isn't it?!'

Dad shook his head. 'Think a little bit closer
to home,' he said.

'**Closer to home . . .**' said Shae. 'Are we going
next door?'

Dad laughed. 'Good guess,' he said, 'but it's **much
better** than that!'

It was Kyah's turn to take a guess. '**I think
we're going on a road trip!**' he said. 'All the

way around Australia! Although we'll **have to go really fast** if we're going to do it in only two weeks...'

'And we wouldn't have time to stop anywhere— that **doesn't sound like much of a holiday**,' I said.

'Alright,' Dad said, '**I don't think you're going to guess** what we're doing.'

'**What <u>are</u> we doing?**' we all asked.

'Straight after school on Friday,' Dad started, 'we're

going to the airport-'

'**Oh, yeaaaaahhhhh!**' said Kyah, who

got up and started running around the dining table.

Shae was **jumping up and down**, and I joined in.

None of us had ever been anywhere by plane, so we

were **super excited** even before Dad told us where

we were going!

'Well, good on you for being so enthusiastic,' Dad said, 'about **going to collect your great aunt Elsie** who's flying in for the holidays.'

'Whaaaaaaaaaaat?!' we all said.

'That's why we're going to the airport?!' I said.

'**We're not actually flying anywhere ourselves?**' said Kyah.

'**Who's great aunt Elsie?**' said Shae.

Dad and Mum thought this was all **<u>very</u> funny**.

Finally, Dad looked over at Mum. They nodded to each other.

'Sorry, boys. Dad joke,' said Dad. He looked at Mum.

Mum said, 'Pack your bags, **we're going to Sunshine Island**!'

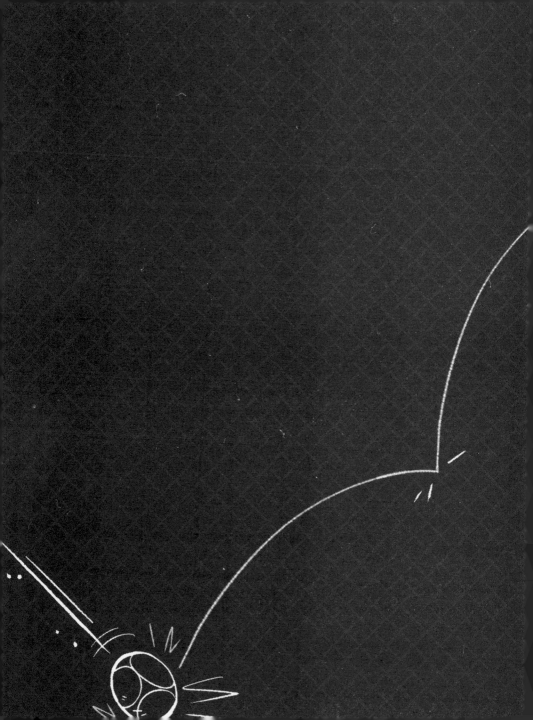

CHAPTER 3

Kyah and Shae went off to pack their bags straight-away, even though we weren't going anywhere for four more days! We were all **really excited**, but deep down, I was still **a tiny bit disappointed** I wouldn't be able to go to the soccer camp.

I knew it was going to be great fun to fly in a plane, and have a holiday with Mum and Dad and Kyah and Shae. I knew there'd be fun stuff to do on the island, but I wasn't sure how much soccer I was going to be able to play, or even watch. I went to check it out on the internet.

And guess what? **Bad news!** Sunshine Island didn't have a pro soccer league! Even worse, it seemed like there weren't any playing fields—at all! It was just hotels and places to eat and beaches everywhere. How could I keep working on my game? **What if I lost my soccer skills!** This holiday wasn't looking that great to me after all . . .

'Don't be ridiculous!' said Sienna. **'It sounds like the best fun ever!'**

'Yeah, you can go swimming, and snorkelling . . .' said Mike.

'Or surfing . . .' said Ricardo.

'Or just hang out on the beach!' said Millie.

We were at training before school—and **my friends thought I was crazy** for thinking that I'd lose my skills in just two weeks.

Hacker and Studs thought so too.

'Get real, Tiny Timmy!' said Studs.

'I sometimes go months without kicking a ball.

Or actually doing any training at all. Or running.

And **do you think that affects my high-level skills**?'

Before I could say anything, he continued,

'No way! I'm still at the very top of my game!'

'Yeah,' said Hacker, 'I don't train and I don't even

have to watch what I eat, but **when I get out on**

the field—magic.'

Wow, these guys were unbelievable!

At the end of training Coach Roach called everyone in to tell us he was planning some **training sessions in the holidays**, so that we'd be ready to go as soon as school started up again in two weeks.

Even after everything my friends had said, I felt **even <u>more</u> disappointed** knowing that I'd miss these holiday training sessions!

'I assume the sessions are optional?' asked Studs.

'Of course,' said Coach Roach.

'Just as well,' said Studs. 'As we've just been explaining to some of our less-talented teammates, Hacker and I **don't have to work quite as hard** as the average player in order to stay at the top of our game.'

'Whatever you like,' said Coach Roach. 'But you might find your game would improve if you **put some more effort in**.'

'**Improve!**' said Studs. 'How much better could we get?'

'Yeah,' said Hacker, 'it's **practically impossible** for us to get any better.'

Some of us laughed.

'**Because we're already so good,**' Hacker explained.

'Anyway, Coach,' Studs continued, 'you don't have to worry. Hacker and I have arranged tactics sessions every day at my house—**playing video games**.'

'And some of them are actually **soccer** **video games**,' added Hacker.

When Studs and Hacker had finished mucking around, I went to tell Coach Roach that I'd be away with my family and that **I'd miss the holiday training sessions**.

'How fantastic!' said Coach Roach. **You'll have a great time**, I'm sure.'

'Yes, but **I'm worried I'll get rusty**. Maybe even lose my skills!' I said.

'No chance,' Coach Roach laughed. 'You can't lose everything you've worked for in the space of two weeks! In any case,' Coach went on, 'if I know you, I'm sure you'll be able to come up with some **creative ways to train** while you're away.'

I hadn't thought about it that way, but Coach was right! If I could fit a ball in my luggage, I'd be fine—**I could practise anywhere!**

CHAPTER 4

The next few days at school were good fun! Our tests were over, and we had the **holidays to look forward** ➡ **to**. We got to watch some movies and even had some of our classes outside in the playground! **Why couldn't school <u>always</u> be like this?!**

Before we knew it, it was the last day of term. We had **one last training session** with Coach Roach at lunchtime, and as a **fun way to finish up** before

the break he let us have shooting practice for the

whole session.

We tried all sorts of

shots: with the **inside**

of the foot,

with the **outside of the foot**,

volleys,

bicycle kicks,

scorpion kicks, everything!

Studs even tried a **rabona**— where you wrap your kicking leg around the outside of your standing leg—but ended up **tripping himself** and falling flat on his face.

Why couldn't training <u>always</u> be like this?!

After that, we just had to get through the afternoon and then it was **HOLIDAY TIME**.

The only problem was, for our last lesson of the term we had a guest speaker in to talk to us about **the history of CARPET** and it seemed to be taking **f-o-r-e-v-e-r**!

We all watched the minutes and the seconds slowly tick down until finally the bell rang for the end of the day. **Wooo-hooooooo!** No more school for **two whole weeks**!

At the school gates we said goodbye to each other.

'Have fun, Tim,' said Sienna. 'You're going to have **the best time ever**!'

'Yeah, I know,' I replied. 'But I still kind of **wish I could go to the soccer camp**. You'll have to tell me all about it when I get back—I know you're going to love it! You too, Mike and Ricardo—at the end of the holidays **you're going to be at the top of your game** after all the practice you'll have done. I'm jealous!'

'Tim, **if anyone's going to be jealous it'll be us** of you and Millie on your overseas holidays!' Ricardo said, and Mike nodded. **'Have fun, both of you!'**

'I know I will,' said Millie. 'And I'll miss you guys!'

Studs and Hacker were walking by.

'**Oh, boo-hoo,**' said Studs. 'Can you believe Tiny

Timmy and his little friends, Hacker? They won't see

each other for a measly two weeks and it's like they're

never going to see each other again ever!'

'Yeah, hand me a tissue,' said Hacker. 'It's bringing

a tear to my eye.'

'Whatever!' I said. '**I'll miss you guys, too**,

believe it or not. See everyone in two weeks!'

We all gave each other a wave and with that, we

were now **officially on holiday**!

When we were back home, Mum handed me a piece of

paper. I took a look:

T-shirts

Shorts

Thongs

Sneakers

Underwear

Jumper

Toothbrush

'What's this?' I asked.

'It's a list of **all the things you need to pack** for our trip,' said Mum. 'I've been asking you to start packing your bag for days, so hopefully this will help you get it done.'

'That's great,' I said, 'but **you left out the most important thing**!' I picked up Mum's pen, made a change to the list, and handed it back:

T-shirts
Shorts
Thongs
Sneakers
Underwear
Jumper
Toothbrush
SOCCER BALL

'Very funny,' said Mum. 'But that's fine. Include your soccer ball—and all the other things on the list—**just please make sure you're packed** and ready to go tomorrow morning!'

I nodded and ran off to pack my bag—making sure

that **the ball went in first** and everything else

was packed around it, so that it was **well and truly**

protected! I couldn't fit my jumper in, but who

needs a jumper on an island holiday anyway?

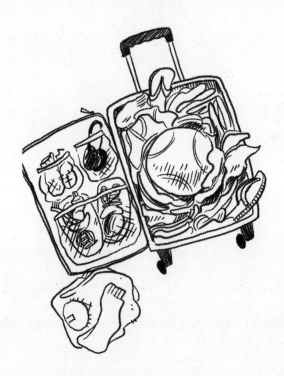

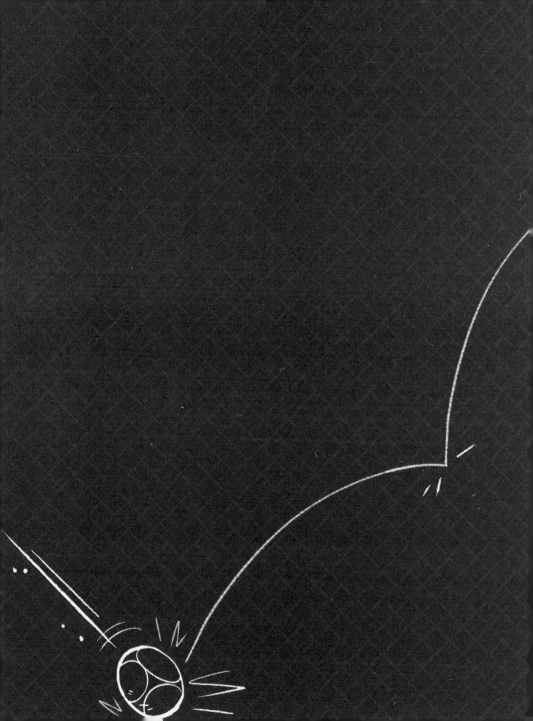

CHAPTER 5

It turned out that **I needed a jumper** on an island holiday! Why hadn't I listened to Mum?! When we landed at Sunshine Island the people at the airport told us that a storm had come in the night before and the weather had got **unexpectedly cold**. I hoped it would warm up, and soon!

The cold weather **wasn't the worst thing** that happened when we arrived, but I'll get to that later . . .

The plane trip itself had been **heaps of fun**!
We got up really early to catch the taxi to the airport,
which actually wasn't that much fun, but from then on
it was **all <u>super</u> exciting**!

Kyah set the alarm off at security and had to go
through the machine twice because he had some coins
in his pockets that he forgot to empty!

Just **getting on the plane** and sitting in our seats was exciting, and then when the plane started to move we were practically **jUmping in our seats**! Just as well we had our seatbelts fastened . . .

And then when the plane **got up to top speed and actually** *took off*, we all just about lost our minds! It was amazing!

One minute we were on the ground, the next we were **way UP in the air**, looking down on where we'd just been! It was so much fun, I wanted to do it again and again!

That is until **we hit some turbulence** and got **bumped around** a bit. That wasn't so much fun, and it got **a bit messy**–that's all I'll say about that!

But then when we felt **better** again, we had all the free drinks we wanted! It was endless! Shae and I thought it was the best thing ever, but Kyah wasn't so sure—mostly because we had to **keep climbing past him** to get to the bathroom.

And then the **very best thing of all** was when we actually landed—how amazing was that!

I thought the pilot must have <u>**super**</u> **skills** to land the big plane on just a skinny bit of runway—it was kind of like a top player finding the corner of the net with a free kick from way out!

Then after we landed, even **getting our bags** off the baggage carousel was exciting! We tried to guess whose bag would come out first—Kyah's was first, mine was last—and then **get through the scrum of people** to pick them off the belt before they disappeared again!

When I collected my bag, it **looked a bit different**. It didn't seem quite as stuffed as when I'd packed it. I opened it up, and **that's when the fun stopped**...

'Whaaaaaat?!' I shouted. **'My soccer ball has popped!'**

This was a disaster! **How was I going to work on my skills now?!**

And <u>now</u> you know why being cold wasn't the worst thing that happened when we landed!

So the ball popped because of the pressure in the plane. It turns out I should have taken the air out of it before we got on, but who knew? I'd actually **pumped it UP** before we flew so it'd last the whole trip away without me needing to bring my pump.

Aaaaargh!

Anyway, after this **huge disappointment** we went to the place we were staying. And I have to say—**it was pretty great!** Two bedrooms, a loungeroom and a kitchen. All nice and new, and looking out over the beach!

The sun was out and the weather was warming up, too, so we went to have a run on the sand. **I brought my ball,** even though it had **popped and was totally floppy**. It was never easy dribbling a ball on sand, and it was doubly hard **now there was no air in it**!

Still, it was **better than nothing**. And even though Kyah wanted to explore the island, Shae wanted to play in the sand, and Mum and Dad just wanted to relax, I got everyone to join in **a game of BEACH SOCCER**!

We made some goalposts out of sand. Shae was in charge and I'm pretty sure it was his favourite part of the whole day. When he finally called out 'Ready!', it was **time to play**!

Shae and I were up against Mum, Dad and Kyah. **The teams weren't even,** but that was OK, because Dad didn't really move from his chair—he just **waved a leg at the ball** if it came near him.

That kind of evened up the teams, but then Shae decided he wouldn't go anywhere near the left wing because **there were some jellyfish** washed up over on that side of the pitch.

This left me with **a lot of ground to cover**, and Kyah and Mum were able to double-team me because it was just about **impossible to switch the play** back over to Shae's side. Every time I tried to pass it to him **the ball just plonked in the sand** a few metres away!

After one of these turnovers, Kyah was able to

collect the ball and race up and **dribble the ball**

through our goal. Shae and I couldn't catch him—

his **legs were too l-o-o-o-n-g** and it was hard

for us to run fast on the sand. And after that, it was just

about **game over** . . .

The tide came in and washed one set of goalposts away. **'Nooooooo,'** said Shae, who was sad to see his works of art destroyed. After that, he lost interest in the game, Mum went to the beachside markets, and then **finally a pelican swooped down**, grabbed what was left of the ball and **dropped it on a ship** way out in the ocean.

'You're going to need a new ball, bro,'

said Kyah.

I nodded. **'You guys win,** 1-0,' I said.

'Hooray!' said Dad from under his hat.

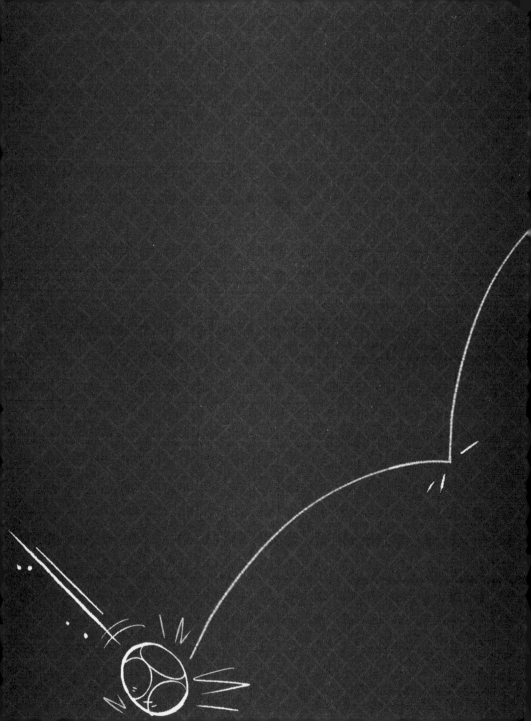

CHAPTER 6

Now that I didn't have even a busted soccer ball, I was going to have to think of some **other ways to train** and make sure I didn't lose my skills!

We ran around the hotel playing **sock soccer**, using rolled-up socks for the ball, just like we did at home. And it was **THE BEST place to play**! We started in our room, ran through the hallways and in the lift, and then even down in the lobby.

We were dribbling around the hotel guests and then I **aimed a shot at the goal**, which was the check-in desk. My shot was just a **tiny bit high** and it clonked into the hotel manager. After that it was time for us to run back to our room, and to **think of a new game to play**!

The next day I was walking near the beach, through the palm trees, wondering how I was going to be able to train. Just then **a coconut fĕll** out of one of the trees and landed right next to me, and **I knew just what to do**!

There were a bunch of coconuts laying around. I knew they were pretty **hard and heavy**, so I chose one that was round like a soccer ball, but not too big— **I didn't want to br**e**ak my foot** when I kicked it! Even so, I'd still have to be careful, especially since I wasn't wearing any shoes.

Down on the beach there were some surfboards for hire, sticking up out of the sand. They were lined up in rows, **perfect for dribbling in**

and out of! I started kicking the coconut, and it wasn't hurting my foot as long as I used the right technique.

I started **running a bit ⹀ faster**, moving quickly around the surfboards while I dribbled the coconut. This was a great training drill, and **I didn't even need a soccer ball** to do it! The guy looking after the surfboard rentals thought so too, and after I'd done another run-through at full speed, he gave me a clap and called out, **'Nice soccer skills!'**

'Thanks!' I said, and flicked the ball up high and **headed it to go into a juggle**.

BIG MISTAKE!

It turns out it was OK to dribble a coconut, **but it was <u>not</u> OK to head it**! I should have known better, but I was kind of showing off. Anyway, I was happy that I'd been able to do some training, but **not so happy that I had a big bump on my head** to show for it!

I needed to find another way to train. A softer way!

That night, **I grabbed the shower cap** from the bathroom and filled it with ice cubes so I could use it as an icepack to help the bump on my head go down. **Then it came to me!** If I could put ice in the shower cap, I could put other stuff in it! All I'd need to do was tape it up and then **I could use it as a ball**!

I just needed to work out what to stuff it with . . .

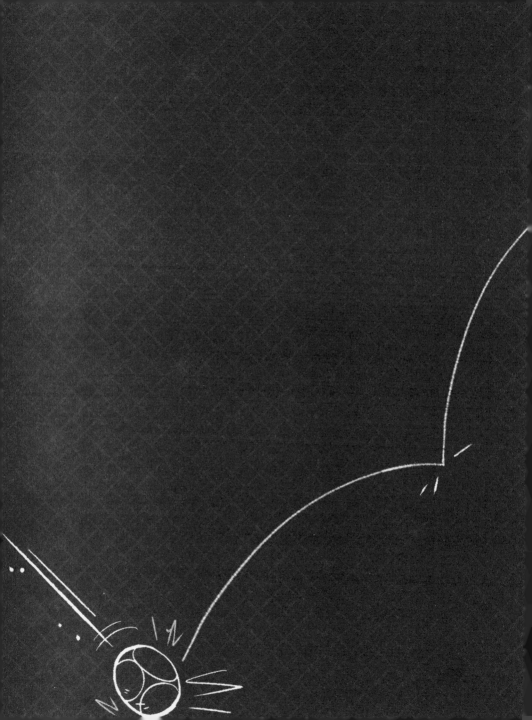

The next day I took my 'ball' over to the beach. Earlier that morning, I'd looked around until I'd found exactly the right stuffing to use—just **some things that were lying around** that weren't going to be used for the rest of the trip.

I thought I'd done a really good job—the only problem I had was when Mum called out from the bathroom, **'Where's my shower cap?!'**

Oops, sorry Mum . . .

As I was **dribbling my shower-cap ball**

along the beach past a row of cafés, I noticed two

palm trees away from the other trees, a few metres

apart from each other. Just about the width of a goal—

perfect for shooting practice!

I moved the ball into position, took a few steps back, ran in and sent it **sailing between the posts**. Goal! This shooting drill was **going to work out fine**!

I took a few more shots, each time from a different angle and a bit further out. I missed a couple of times, but most went right through the middle of the trees. After a while, a lot of the people in the cafés saw what I was doing and were **giving me a cheer** whenever I scored a goal.

That was fine—having an audience made me **concentrate even more**. For my next kick, I took the ball to a really tight angle. I ran in, kicked it, and the ball . . . **crashed into the post**. So close!

The crowd in the café gave a big 'ooh'. I looked over and shrugged, as if to say 'you can't win them all'. The next second, though, **I could hear some laughs**, and then a lot of laughs, and a girl about my age said, **'Oooh, gross!'**

My shot wasn't that bad! It hit the post! But then I saw **that was actually the problem . . .**

I'd stuffed my used underpants and socks in the shower cap to make the ball. And when the ball hit the tree, it busted open—and **all my undies had fallen out all over the place**. How embarrassing!

I quickly ran and grabbed up my undies and what was left of the shower cap. I could hear the crowd **giving me another cheer** as I jogged back towards our hotel—at least **I'd given them some entertainment** as they ate their breakfast!

After that I tried to do some training that **didn't**

need a ball!

I practised my leap, and at the same time

helped out the lifeguards doing beach patrol, by

jumping up ↑**high**↑ to see if there were any sharks

around or swimmers in trouble.

Then to work on my *speed* and agility
I ran as fast as I could along the beach, at the point
where the waves were coming in and rolling up onto
the sand. It was kind of like the water was a defender,
so I **zig-zagged and jumped**, making sure it
didn't touch my feet.

I thought it would be good to work on my fitness, too. There were some sand dunes nearby, so **I ran up the hills** until I was well and truly out of breath. I knew this was great exercise, but it was **much more fun coming back down**!

As well as my training, we all did some other **really cool stuff**, too.

We went snorkelling, and **Shae said he saw a giant squid**! We didn't believe him of course, but we did see some amazing fish, and even some turtles swimming around.

We had a bike race along the track that went around the island. **Mum couldn't believe it** when Kyah, Shae and I beat her and Dad.

Mum did beat us all at mini golf, though. I think she'd been practising . . .

It had been **great spending time together as a family**, and doing lots of stuff that we didn't get a chance to do very much at home. But after all that, I really just **wanted to kick a ball around**!

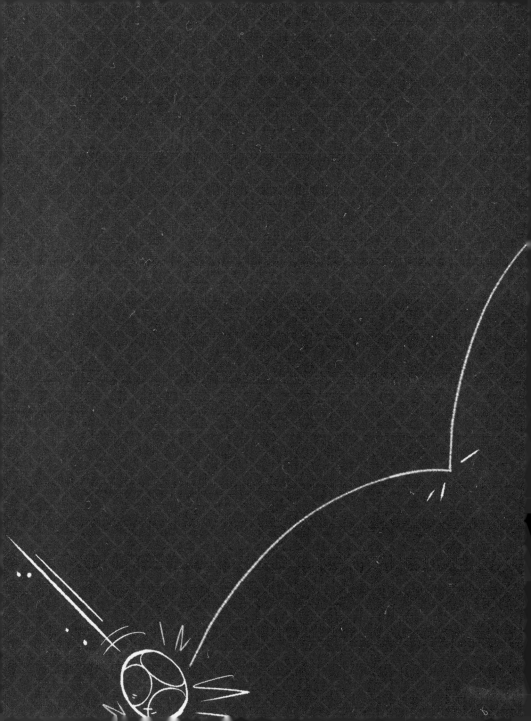

CHAPTER 8

The next morning we all went to the beach. Kyah was going surfing, Shae was building things in the sand, and I went along to have a swim. **This was good exercise,** and also good fun.

And then **my ears pricked up** as I heard a familiar sound. A sound I'd know anywhere: thonk, thonk, thonk, thonk. I turned around and there it was...

a kid juggling a soccer ball!

I waved and called out. The kid got distracted and **lost control of the ball**, which shot off into the water. I waded over and grabbed it. I threw the ball to him and **he headed it back at me**! So I headed it back to him, and we **kept the ball in the air** while he waded into the shallow water.

This wasn't easy, so **I could tell he had some pretty good skills**. At the end of the game, I asked him his name.

'I'm Nic,' he said. 'Nice to meet you!'

'I'm Tim,' I said. 'Where are you from?'

'I live here on the island with my brother and sister and my Dad. Hey, how did you get to be such a good header of the ball?'

'Lots and lots of practice!' I said. 'I play all the time at home for my team, the **LIONS**, and my rep team, the **TIGERS**, and we have heaps of training sessions, and pretty much **any other time I have I spend practising** with my friends or my brothers or on my own.'

'Wow,' said Nic. 'I practise all the time, but **we don't have enough kids** living here on the island to have a league. We hardly have enough for one team!'

How bad would that be?! All those skills, and no chance to use them in any proper games!

'That's terrible!' I said. 'I knew there were no pro teams here, but I didn't know there **weren't any teams at all**!'

'Yeah, it's bad—but **at least I didn't show my dirty underwear** to half the island,' said Nic with a grin. 'Bet you can't get the ball off me!' he called as he went racing up the beach, dribbling the ball.

News sure travelled fast around here!

I chased after Nic and tried to take the ball off him, but he was really fast and was a great dribbler, too. I finally managed to get it off him and then it was my turn to keep the ball away from Nic. This was more like it—**soccer training with an actual soccer ball!**

It started to get dark, and we were tired, so we decided to head back to our families—Nic to his home and me to our hotel.

'See you back here tomorrow?' I asked.

'Definitely!' said Nic. 'Bring your brothers and we can have **a game of three-on-three**!'

'Awesome!' I said. 'See you then!'

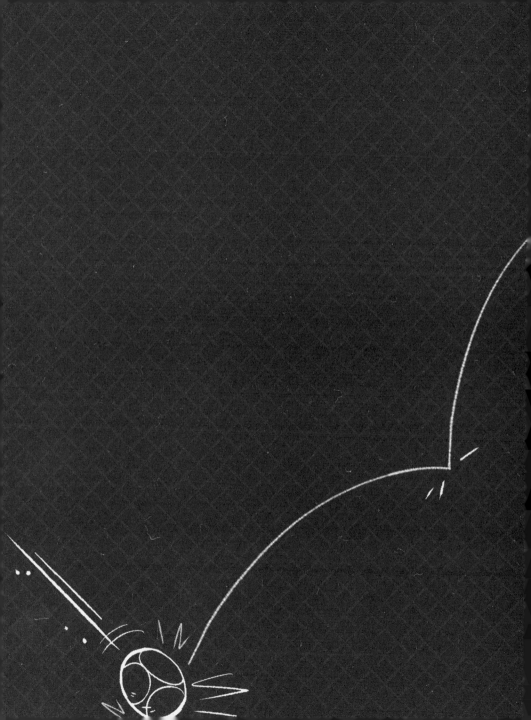

CHAPTER 9

We all met up the next day as planned. Shae did a great job with the goalposts again, and then we got stuck into **a high-level game** of three-on-three beach soccer!

Nic's brother Thomas was around the same age as Kyah, and his sister, Emilie, was Shae's age. **And they could all play!** How did they get so good without being on a proper team?!

Emilie scored the first goal after Nic had held the ball up and flicked it over to where she was standing unmarked. Emilie controlled it easily and kicked the ball through the posts.

Then Nic scored a great solo goal after dribbling around all three of us, and straight after that **Thomas lobbed the ball** over Kyah and into the goal. They were really **teaching us a beach soccer lesson**!

We scored a nice goal, and then another, but Nic's team kept scoring too, and we were **never able to catch up**. The game kind of finished when Emilie and Shae stopped playing to make a mermaid sand sculpture. We'd had a really good game, but **the Cahill boys had lost this one**!

'You guys were too good today,' I said. 'Well played!'

'Must have been our home-field advantage,' replied Nic. 'When it comes to beach soccer **we really know what we're doing**. Maybe you guys would win if we played on grass.'

'Maybe,' I said, nodding. 'It's a bit different, but you **still need heaps of skill** to play on the sand— maybe even more skill!'

'All I know for sure is that this is **the <u>best</u> game we've had in ages**,' said Nic.

'Maybe the best ever!' added Thomas.

'How good would it be if we could play five-on-five?' said Kyah.

Everyone was quick to agree.

'Well what about if we could play eleven-on-eleven—like **a proper game, with full teams**!' I said. 'Now **<u>that</u> would be awesome**!'

'It would be sooooo awesome,' said Nic. 'But **how could it happen**? Like I said, there are no teams here, and the three-on-three game we just played was the most people we've played with for ages.'

Thomas agreed. 'It would be great, but I can't see how it would be possible.'

'Don't worry,' I said. **'I have a few ideas!'**

I'd seen **heaps of kids** here on holiday with their families. I was sure at least some of them would want to play some beach soccer. We just **needed to get the word out** that there was going to be a game, and to get them **all together in the same place at the same time**!

★ 98 ★

We made some fliers:

THE MOST EPIC BEACH SOCCER GAME EVER

Calling all kids to come and play beach soccer!

Bring your sister, bring your brother,
bring your cousin, bring your friend!

We need eleven against eleven, so that our
friends can see what it's like.

When: Saturday at 12 o'clock

Where: the beach

See everybody then!

We put the **fliers on the noticeboard** at our hotel. The hotel manager was happy to spread the word, too—just as long as we didn't play in the lobby! **We gave fliers to the other hotels** near us as well.

We walked along the beachfront and handed out fliers to **all the cafés and restaurants**, too. Heaps of people had been watching when I'd been practising last week, so I thought there should be a **good crowd to watch our big game** on Saturday.

We just needed to make sure we had enough players so there **would actually <u>be</u> a big game**!

While we were there near the beach, I went over to see **my friends on beach patrol**. A moment later, an announcement came over the loudspeaker:

'Attention please, attention please.'

Everyone **stopped what they were doing**.

Was there a shark alert? Or a dangerous current?

'Please note that all kids are invited to **the most epic beach soccer game ever**, this Saturday at 12 o'clock. Everybody welcome!'

Thanks beach patrol guys! We were pretty sure that we'd **got the word out** to most of the kids on the island. Now we just needed to wait until Saturday to see if we'd have enough players for **eleven against eleven**!

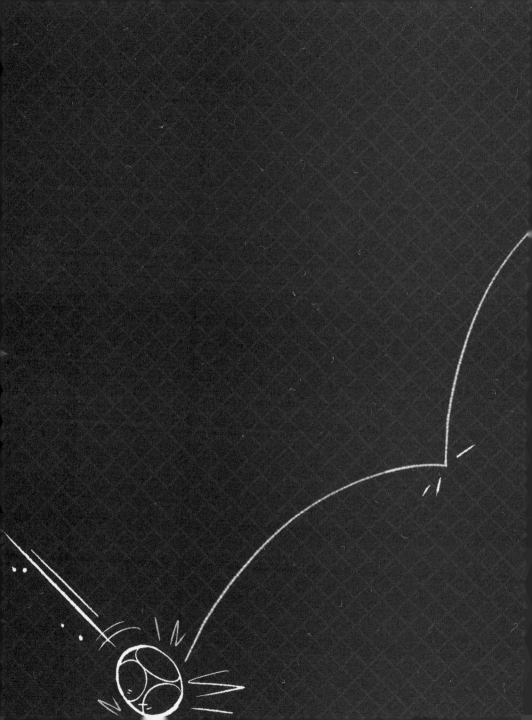

CHAPTER 10

We met at the beach early on Saturday morning. Everyone was excited to get going!

We got busy **measuring out the pitch**. Kyah and Thomas and Nic and I started marking out the lines, while Shae and Emilie began **working on the goalposts**.

'Are you sure the tide's not going to come in and wash everything away?' asked Shae.

'One hundred percent sure,' said Nic. '**We'll be able to play our game** before the tide comes back in.'

That was good enough for Shae, who went back to making the goalposts.

It took us more than an hour, but when we were done we had **the best-looking beach soccer pitch** that there had ever been! Which was just the way it should be—**we <u>couldn't</u> play** the most epic beach soccer match ever on just any old patch of sand!

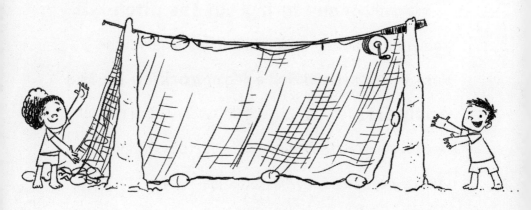

We'd done a good job marking the lines, but Shae and Emilie's goalposts were **a thing of real beauty**! The posts came up to head height, they'd used fishing rods to make the crossbars, and then they'd draped fishing nets over the top. They looked **as good as real soccer goals**!

With the pitch ready to go, all we had to do now was wait for all the kids to come!

We waited. **And we waited some more.** The only kid who came was the girl from the café, who saw me, called out, **'Dirty undies boy,'** then ran back to her mum and dad. Where was everybody?! It was nearly 12 o'clock!

To fill in some time, as well as to warm up for the game that we hoped was still going to happen, we kicked the ball around in a circle up near the palm trees—**we didn't want to mess up the pitch** before we played on it for real. I kicked the ball to Kyah, and it **bounced off a coconut** and ran away behind him.

A kid trapped the ball and called out, 'Is this yours?'

He dribbled the ball up to where we were playing, and continued, 'And is this where the epic game is happening? It **doesn't look very epic** right now.'

'It's not 12 o'clock yet,' I said.

'Yes, it is,' he said, **pointing**  **to his watch**.

Oh, no! It looked like our epic game was an **epic fizzer**!

'Maybe everyone's going to come a little bit late,' I said. 'Anyway, **do you want to play**?'

'I'd love to!' he said. 'My name's Hugo.'

We all said hi and introduced ourselves.

'I'm here from Spain, on holiday with my parents,' Hugo said, 'and I've **been wanting to play** the whole time I've been on the island. I was **really excited** when I heard there was going to be a game on today.'

'Me too!' said a girl who'd just been swimming and walked up the beach towards us. 'My name's Astrid, and I'm from Norway. You've made a beautiful pitch—it would **be a shame not to play on it**!'

'I agree!' said a boy who'd jogged over from the canoe rental stand. **'Let's play!'**

That was Lucas, on holiday from Sweden, and there was Junichi from Japan, and Shelby from America, and Anna from Germany—**kids were coming from everywhere now!** From the cafés and restaurants, from the hotels, from the beach and the bike tracks, all wanting to play! It looked like **we might just get to play an epic game**, after all!

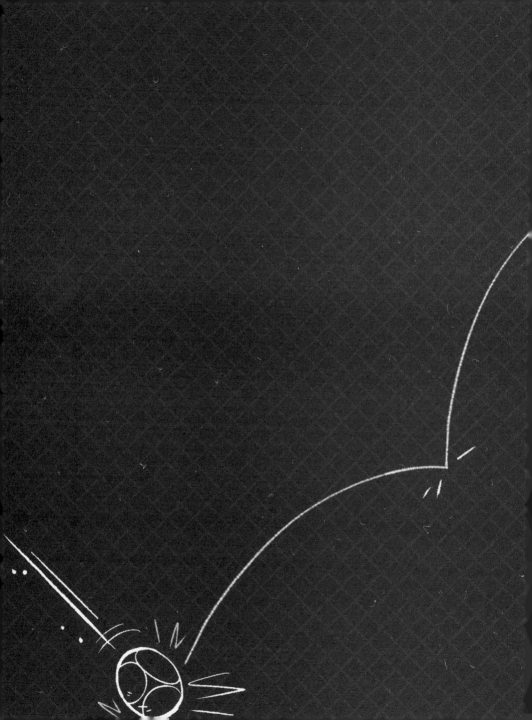

CHAPTER 11

★

We'd really wanted to play with eleven against eleven, so Nic and his family could see what it was like to **play with two full teams**. But that didn't happen.

It was even <u>more</u> epic than that!

We started playing with my brothers and I plus Nic's family against the rest. Then as everyone who wanted to play arrived at the beach, we added players to each side until **I lost count of how many** were

playing. We definitely had enough players for at least

three full teams, maybe even four!

On top of that, we had everyone's parents watching on from the beach and the cafés—it was a ready-made crowd **to cheer us on** and make it an amazing atmosphere. **It was bigger than epic!**

With so many players on each team it was actually **really hard to score goals**—too many defenders to get past! Nic did manage to **score a top-class goal** when he dribbled around what seemed to be about ten players before shooting it into the bottom corner.

The other team scrambled a goal to make it 1-1, and with the tide on its way back in Nic called out,

'Next goal wins!'

It didn't look like either team was going to be able to win it—there were just **too many bodies around the ball**! Then I thought about it and realised there was much **more space in the air** than on the sand! I pointed to my head and Nic knew just what to do.

I made a run towards the posts and Nic flicked the ball **Up over the top** of everyone. **I jUmped higher** than the kid who was playing goalkeeper for the other team, and nodded the ball between the posts. **GOAL!**

That meant our team won the game, but **that really wasn't the point** of today. Nic finally had a chance to play a game with a full team—even more than a full team, actually—and while it wasn't on grass, it was still good experience.

I hoped he'd get the chance to play some organised soccer soon—**it'd be a shame to waste all those skills!**

On top of that, we'd wanted **the most epic beach soccer game ever**, and we reckoned that's exactly what we got! It had been heaps of fun, and the **perfect way to finish up our holiday**.

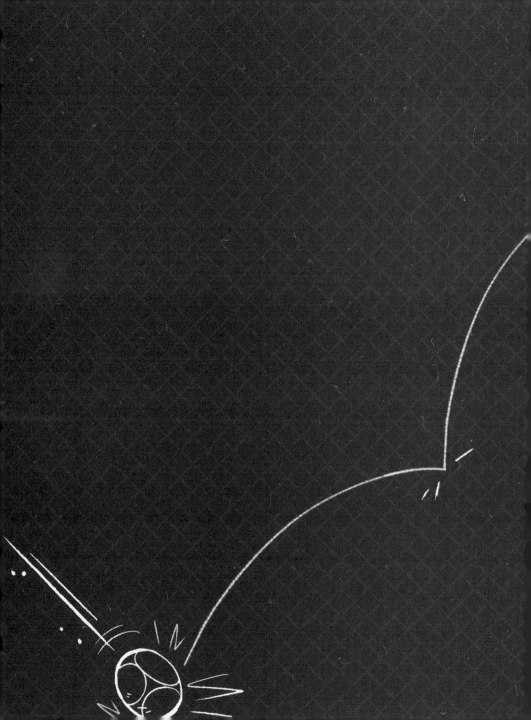

CHAPTER 12

The next morning at the airport, Mum asked us if we'd enjoyed our trip.

'**Sure did!**' we all shouted.

'What was your favourite part?' asked Dad.

'**Surfing and bike riding,**' said Kyah.

'I liked snorkelling the most,' said Shae. '**And making the goalposts.**'

'Oh,' said Dad. 'What about the game yesterday?'

'That was good,' said Shae. 'But making the goalposts was better.'

'Fair enough,' said Dad, with a chuckle.

'I liked the whole holiday,' I said. 'Especially the game at the end—**that was the best!'**

'So you're glad you came along with us, even though you **missed out on the soccer camp**?' asked Mum.

'Definitely!' I said. '**I was able to keep working on my skills**—even without a ball! It was just as good as being at camp—no, better! I got to do some **fun stuff with you guys**, and to **meet kids from all over the world**, and I **made a good friend**, too.'

'Hey, Tim!'

It was Nic! 'What are you doing here?' I asked.

'I just wanted to say goodbye again, and thanks for helping to organise the epic game yesterday. I told Dad all about it and he says **we should do it every year**—like a great big beach-soccer carnival! He said he'd help organise it.'

'That's awesome!' I said. **'Maybe we can come back next year!'** I looked at Mum and Dad.

'Sounds like a plan,' said Mum, who'd had a really good holiday, too.

Dad nodded—he **didn't have much choice**!

Our flight got called for boarding, so we gave Nic a final wave.

'See you again soon,' I called, and we made our way to the plane.

COLLECT THEM ALL!

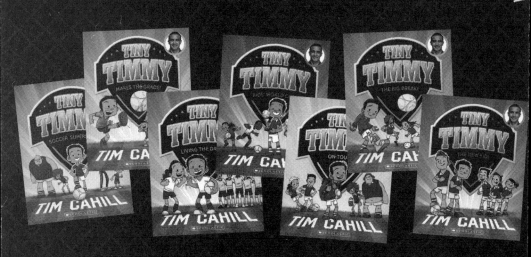

Look out for more

books coming soon!